DO NOT DISTURB

NANCY TAFURI

GREENWILLOW BOOKS · NEW YORK

FOR SUSAN

The full-color art was done in black line with
colored inks and dyes. The typeface is Leawood.

Copyright © 1987 by Nancy Tafuri. All rights
reserved. No part of this book may be reproduced
or utilized in any form or by any means,
electronic or mechanical, including photocopying,
recording or by any information storage and
retrieval system, without permission in writing
from the Publisher, Greenwillow Books, a
division of William Morrow & Company, Inc.,
105 Madison Avenue, New York, N.Y. 10016.

Printed in Hong Kong by
South China Printing Co.
First Edition   10 9 8 7 6 5 4 3 2 1

Library of Congress Cataloging-in-Publication Data

Tafuri, Nancy.   Do not disturb.
Summary: The movements and actions of a family camping in the woods
cause the forest creatures to also move, scurry, and make noise.
[1. Camping—Fiction.   2. Animals—Fiction.   3. Stories without words]
I. Title.   PZ7.T117Do 1987   [E]   86-357
ISBN 0-688-06541-4   ISBN 0-688-06542-2 (lib. bdg.)

It was the first day

of summer...

Tafuri, Nancy   SUMMER   JJ
Do not disturb